Samuel French Actin

26 Pebbles

by Eric Ulloa

SAMUELFRENCH.COM   SAMUELFRENCH.CO.UK

MUSIC USE NOTE

Licensees are solely responsible for obtaining formal written permission from copyright owners to use copyrighted music in the performance of this play and are strongly cautioned to do so. If no such permission is obtained by the licensee, then the licensee must use only original music that the licensee owns and controls. Licensees are solely responsible and liable for all music clearances and shall indemnify the copyright owners of the play(s) and their licensing agent, Samuel French, against any costs, expenses, losses and liabilities arising from the use of music by licensees. Please contact the appropriate music licensing authority in your territory for the rights to any incidental music.

IMPORTANT BILLING AND CREDIT REQUIREMENTS

If you have obtained performance rights to this title, please refer to your licensing agreement for important billing and credit requirements.

26 PEBBLES had its world premiere at The Human Race Theatre Company in Dayton, Ohio on February 4, 2017. The artistic director was Kevin Moore, and the director was Igor Goldin. The cast was as follows:

ACTOR 1	Caitlin McWethy
ACTOR 2	Jason Podplesky
ACTOR 3	Scott Hunt
ACTOR 4	Gina Handy
ACTOR 5	Christine Brunner
ACTOR 6	Jennifer Joplin

CHARACTERS

Actor 1 – female, plays:

JENN – (thirty-five) Mother to six-year-old son, and wife to Michael. Lives in Sandy Hook.

CARLA – (forty) Married mother of two, retired airline pilot who lives on a farm and enjoys the simple life.

Actor 2 – male, plays:

MICHAEL – (thirty-five) Father of six-year-old son and married to Jenn. Lives in Sandy Hook.

DARREN – (forty-five) Father of two boys and married to Georgia. Suffers from PTSD.

BILL – (sixty) Married to Carole and father to Sally. Retired blue-collar worker with a salt of the earth mentality. Carole's rock.

FATHER WEISS – (fifty-five) Monsignor of the Catholic church and Christian spiritual leader to the community. A bit worn out and weary by the responsibilities thrust into his life on 12/14.

Actor 3 – male, plays:

JOE – (thirty-five) Former art teacher at Sandy Hook Elementary School.

CHRIS – (forty) Works in city hall and oversaw the collection of gifts after 12/14. A straight-talking and "no-nonsense" guy.

RABBI SHAUL PRAVER – (forty-five) Passionate Rabbi and Jewish spiritual leader of the community.

MIKE – (thirty-five) Blue-collar construction worker and contractor born and raised in Sandy Hook.

Actor 4 – female, plays:

YOLIE – (forty) Artistic-minded, divorced mother of one who is passionate about her community and how they can change the future of others.

JERIANN – (forty) Spiritual healer who is new to the community. Opened a healing and angel reading shop with Starr.

SALLY – (thirty-five) Hometown girl who loves her community. Daughter of Carole and Bill.

Actor 5 – female, plays:

GEORGIA – (forty) Australian-born mother of two boys and married to Darren. Newtown is the first home she's made in the U.S. with her family.

KAT – (forty-five) Former factory worker now turned volunteer of incoming gifts to the town. Gravely voiced and tough on the outside but a heart of gold, hug-loving person on the inside.

CARRIE – (forty) Married mother of two girls. Lives in Sandy Hook.

Actor 6 – female, plays:

JULIE – (forty) Married mother of two. Lives in Sandy Hook.

STARR – (fifty) Angel reader who is born and bred in the community, and a bit quirky. She opened a healing and angel reading shop with Jeriann.

CAROLE – (sixty) Tough, salt of the earth human resources director of Newtown. She is "no-nonsense" and has a tremendous love of her town and its constituents. She is married to Bill and mother to Sally.

SETTING

A town hall meeting in Newtown, Connecticut

TIME

Six months after December 14, 2012

AUTHOR'S NOTES

NOTE ON SET: *26 Pebbles* can be performed as simply as using multiple chalkboards throughout the playing space. These are all written upon and used by the actors throughout the play.

NOTE ON AUDIENCE: Audience members should be given name tags to wear throughout the duration of the show, to establish the concept of a community town hall meeting. The actors would pass them out prior to showtime to establish this feeling. This is not a necessity and is only a suggestion that has worked in past productions. If not used, Jenn's line on page one would read:

> And we need more of that nowadays,
> right...may I ask your name?

(Says the name of the audience member in front of her.)

> See how easy and painless that was?
> Now you try it. Turn to your
> neighbor and say "Hi!"

NOTE ON CAST: The cast is comprised of six people playing a multitude of characters. All six cast members should be dressed in non-descript outfits that can also have name tags affixed to them. The changing of characters will involve the addition of a small accessory and their name tag.

NOTE ON MUSIC: The singing of "Come, Thou Fount of Every Blessing" should be simple and raw, with only the accompaniment of a pre-taped guitar (Licensees should create their own recording).

"COME, THOU FOUNT OF EVERY BLESSING"

COME, THOU FOUNT OF EVERY BLESSING,
TUNE MY HEART TO SING THY GRACE;

STREAMS OF MERCY, NEVER CEASING,

CALL FOR SONGS OF LOUDEST PRAISE.

TEACH ME SOME MELODIOUS SONNET,

SUNG BY FLAMING TONGUES ABOVE.
PRAISE THE MOUNT! I'M FIXED UPON IT,
MOUNT OF THY REDEEMING LOVE.

O TO GRACE HOW GREAT A DEBTOR
DAILY I'M CONSTRAINED TO BE!
LET THY GOODNESS, LIKE A FETTER,

BIND MY WANDERING HEART TO THEE.

PRONE TO WANDER, LORD, I FEEL IT,

PRONE TO LEAVE THE GOD I LOVE;
HERE'S MY HEART, O TAKE AND SEAL IT,
SEAL IT FOR THY COURTS ABOVE.

FOREWORD

"How are you out of vodka? Ugh!"

Those were the words that set me off on this journey. On December 14, 2012, I was bartending a holiday party for a large corporate company trying to scrounge together some last-minute holiday cash in a year that was less than fruitful when it came to performing gigs. Earlier that morning, a mentally disturbed young man walked into an elementary school and killed twenty small children and six adults, yet here an inebriated woman was berating me on the lack of vodka as she simultaneously checked her text messages. I know the world has to continue spinning no matter how dire a moment it just endured, but my god, can't we stop and reflect on the atrocity that just happened for a moment. The holidays came and went, as well as the dark, short days of January and February, and still this horrific tragedy clung heavily to my heart. I watched as the media unplugged their cords and packed up their trucks as the Newtown story was no longer a ratings surge for them. I watched as the hope for gun reform peaked to an all-time high and then watched as hearts broke all over again due to its failure to pass in any form of legislation. By late March, everyone had moved on, and yet my mind couldn't let go of a number of questions. How do people of this town go on from here? Can they erase this mark? Does an incident like this shake your entire spiritual bedrock? I did what we all do when we feel flustered and have no control over a situation – I posted on Facebook...incessantly. I made so much noise on social media that at times it was even deafening to me. And therein lied the inherent problem; it was all just noise. What was I actively doing to create change about something that hit me so hard? It was at that moment that the idea came to me. I had a voice, I had questions and I had the ability to go to Newtown and talk with these people and see what exactly was going on. When I first arrived in Newtown, I had only one interview scheduled and a hotel room booked for a week. My first interview met me on a bench right in front of the library. After a few awkward seconds, we finally got to talking like two people in search of something; she unloaded some of this pain, and I was hungry to understand and accept what had happened here. She then picked up her phone and reached out to some friends about the experience we just had together, and soon that one interview became three...then nine...then fifteen. By the end of it all, I had returned to Newtown on multiple trips and held just over sixty interviews with people from all walks of life within this community. I had been given a home to stay in (someone actually gave me their house one week), fed multiple meals in many different kitchens, and even had dog sitters who watched my dog Bastian while I held these interviews daily. I had become a part of their town, and they had become lifelong friends.

During the initial week, I noticed how quaint and beautiful Newtown was, and how it reminded me of "Grover's Corners." Everyone and everything had its place, and it all seemed almost idyllic until they were thrown this terrible curve ball. And that's when it hit me. I would write a play with a similar structure to *Our Town* and use their own words from these interviews to give insight into how people can and do move forward after tragedy. *26 Pebbles* is not a play about the death of twenty young children and six adults. Those are just the circumstances. *26 Pebbles* is a story of hope and of family and of community. It is a story of the human condition. It's hard to say what I hope people will leave with after seeing *26 Pebbles*. It's tough stuff, I'm not gonna lie about it, it is truly tough stuff...but it's also necessary. We change the channel way too fast in this country and compartmentalize our feelings about a tragedy as soon as we are done dealing with it. We stick a Band-Aid on a broken limb and hope for the best. I guess all I ask for is that you enable audiences to leave the theater and continue to discuss and tell the story of Newtown. Educate them so that they tell their friends and family and neighbors the incredible true story of these people. I am honored to be the one to tell this story to all of you and I am humbled in knowing that you will continue to spread it further.

-Eric Ulloa

For my parents, who gave me this heart...

And for the people of Newtown, who taught me new ways to use it.

"It is better to light a candle than to curse the darkness."
– Old Chinese Proverb

(**JENN** *enters the stage, reading a newspaper.*)

JENN. It's crazy to me that we're on the map. Six months later and our town is still on this national map. Everybody now knows where Newtown is.

> (*Beat.*)

Communities like ours don't just form themselves. A true sense of community comes from strangers wanting to come together and know one another for the greater good of their neighborhood. And we need more of that nowadays, right…

> (*Says the name of the audience member in front of her.*)

See how easy and painless that was? Now you try it. Turn to your neighbor, check out their name tag and say "Hi!"

> (*The audience turns and greets one another.*)

And now we have a community.

> (*The actor playing* **MIKE** *enters.*)

MIKE. You know on the thirteenth, you didn't know where Newtown was or that we had a flagpole, or a creamery, or a parade. Obscure was nice.

> (*He walks offstage.* **JENN** *takes in the moment of awkwardness and then moves forward.*)

JENN. To know where we are, you have to know who we are. So let's wipe the slate clean, because let's face it, he's right. Obscurity was nice.

> (*She takes out a piece of chalk and writes "The Town" on the wall chalkboard.*)

JENN. They say the world is connected through six degrees, but out here in Newtown, it's about one. And if you were born and raised here, everyone is family.

(The actor playing **SALLY** *enters.)*

SALLY. The friends I have, are the friends that I grew up with. I do have a couple of new ones, but most of the friends that I hang out with, I grew up with. And people are like, "Really? Because I don't even talk to anybody I grew up with." But it's...it's...everybody wants to come back, you know?

JENN. How many of you have been out to Newtown?

(Her reaction is based on their answer. Either, "Not many of you, huh?" or "Wow, quite a bit of you!")

Newtown is pretty spread out, but it all comes together at the center of town. And smack-dab in the middle is the flagpole.

(She draws a circle right in the middle of the playing space.)

If you haven't seen it, it's this big huge flagpole with a massive American flag high above the town. Right next to it is Edmond Town Hall.

(She draws a square next to it and labels it "Edmond Town Hall." The lights come up on **CAROLE**. *There is a diagram of how these markings are laid out in the back of this Acting Edition.)*

CAROLE. Edmond Town Hall is the only two-dollar movie theater in the entire state. The town offices used to be there, as you might have guessed, but we had to move them to Fairfield Hills. Just too much bureaucracy to contain within a 1930s building I guess.

JENN. There's also a secret bathroom in there one flight down, that if no one is looking, can be very helpful in case of emergency... But don't tell anyone.

Now, Main Street runs straight through the town.

(She draws a line straight across the playing space.)

And all along it we have churches, restaurants, the library and businesses like the Dana Holcombe House Bed and Breakfast.

(She draws little squares representing these structures and labels them. Lights come up on **GEORGIA** *and* **DARREN**.*)*

GEORGIA. We'd been living in Australia and Darren hadn't been back to see his family here in the states for mostly nineteen years, and so it was time to come back. So we started researching, as I had all this criteria it had to be. It had to be on the coast, and the east coast is closer to Ohio than the west coast, so we'll do the east coast. Um, it had to be no more than an hour from the coast, uh, 'cause, 'cause all Australians live no more than an hour from the coast. We can't cope.

DARREN. Landlocked does not work.

GEORGIA. So I said, "Look, I can't live in Ohio, sorry. I can't live in Ohio under any circumstances.

DARREN. *(Laughing.)* And you had no argument from me did you?

GEORGIA. So we decide we want to be driving distance from New York, but somewhere that was kinda similar to what the kids and us knew, which was kind of a small sleepy town. The very first house that comes up is in a place called Newtown.

Now Newtown is one of my favorite towns in Australia. So, the name, and kind of everything fits, the idea of a "new town." So, I'm all, "Let's research this town." And just everything was like, "Oh wow, it has great schools," "Oh! It has low crime."

DARREN. Where we were living was just zero crime of any kind. They've never even lost a politician to violence. They did however lose one Prime Minister...how'd they lose him?

GEORGIA. *(Laughing.)* He went swimming one day and never came back. They never found him.

DARREN. So we get there and drive into town, see the flagpole and pull up to the Dana Holcombe House. We have this amazing loft upstairs.

GEORGIA. Like a family suite, called the "Americana Room."

DARREN. Which was, ya know, flag bedspread, flag pillowcase, flag carpet, flag pictures and flag mementos on the bookcase. And in Australia, Australians don't, they're not patriotic per se. They don't, they're not flag-waving.

GEORGIA. No, definitely not flag-waving.

DARREN. So on her first night in America, she got to come back and sleep in bed, and drape herself in a flag while looking out the window, because you can see the flagpole and there was this breeze enough so that in the wind it's snapping, ya know, full. You're falling asleep to the red white and blue.

GEORGIA. You wake up the next morning in a jet lag, and you know how sometimes when you wake up somewhere new and you don't really remember where you were? And where you are? So I wake up and there are a thousand American Flags in my face, I'm like, "Okay, we're definitely in America!"

JENN. Now, right off Main Street is Ram's Pasture, which is this beautiful historic field.

(She draws the field.)

Now if you go turn right at the pasture, you'll hit Sugar Street and right up the road is the Creamery.

*(As she begins to draw a circle and label it "The Creamery," lights up on **SALLY**.)*

SALLY. Okay, so the Creamery is, they rallied around the town to save this farm. And it's literally on the other side of here, it's really close, and on this side of the mountain. It's a working dairy farm and they make their own ice cream.

And so, there's a shack there and it's open from noon to ten every night. It's starting April ninth, till like I guess it's cold. And sometimes you go and it's packed and it's this awesome ice cream. And you smell the manure, I mean, it's out in like a dairy farm. It's just one of those things where you're like, "This is Newtown."

KAT. Oh, I'm the Town Hugger.

　　(*Laughs.*)

That's the only title that's been given to me. I'm actually still in the house I was born in. I uh... Brought up in Sandy Hook, uh, most of my life. I'm actually fourth-generation here in town on my mother's side, so stories I could give ya, stories that go back even before my time. Everybody knew everybody, um, everybody watched over everybody's kids. I mean, I have so many moms and dads to this day. Lets see, what else... Um, Pat Lhodra is our first selectman, so I guess that's kind of like our mayor you could say.

BILL. Carole runs the town of Newtown

CAROLE. Oh please, stop. My god I'll lose my job.

BILL. They'll say, they'll say, "Gee, what does she do?" And I tell 'em, well she, she runs the town of Newtown.

SALLY. She does. My mom runs it.

CAROLE. (*To audience.*) No she doesn't!

BILL. Everything one way or another gets passed through Carole. And well, even her boss, ya know? But the beauty of it is, is that she feels comfortable enough to do that.

SALLY. (*Breathes in and looks around.*) There are so many memories just right here! Of playing with the neighborhood kids and sledding in the wintertime. And the bell, the sound of the bell! The bell attached to the side of the house, that was the way Mom got us home.

BILL. It's a bronze bell that was cast at a foundry I worked at, and they gave it to me as a gift when I left, ya know?

CAROLE. And you can hear it all over the neighborhood, and all the kids ran and that was it, it was time for dinner. And if I rang the bell twice...

> *(She gives a look to **SALLY**.)*

JENN. If we were to head back to the flagpole and make a sharp left, you'd find yourself on Church Hill Road.

> *(She draws a line up left from the flagpole and labels it.)*

Follow Church Hill straight up and you'll find yourself smack in the village of Sandy Hook.

> *(She draws the symbol for Sandy Hook and labels it. Lights go down on her and come up on **MIKE**.)*

MIKE. I grew up and went to all the schools here. It's our lifeblood, this town. Been here a long time. Specifically Sandy Hook. Specifically Sandy Hook. It's been Sandy Hook for the most part. We're builders. We do a lot of things, builders and contractors, we're property managers. We own a lot of commercial property that you see here.

STARR. Jeriann and I met at Captain Cooks and we decided we were going to, um, have a, open our first business. And this was not our first choice.

JERIANN. Actually, we were at another space, because I'm not from here. So there was a calling for me. Uh, we looked at another space, on Main Street, and we were sitting down to sign the papers for the lease, and I looked at Starr and the other landlord and I said, "You know, my angels are telling me we just can't do this." So then we ended up here in Sandy Hook. I'm a healer and Starr does angel readings, and there was such a calling to come here.

STARR. We're hoping to help everyone.

> *(She hands a business card to someone in the audience.)*

If you came in and you told me a story, that ya, ya know, and you said, "I'm really confused. I really don't know where I'm going." Myself or Jeriann can sit with you.

JERIANN. Yeah, yeah.

JENN. *(Looking at her work.)* Well, that's about it. As you can see we have our "born and breds," but we're also a town of transplants from all over. The story pretty much tells itself from this point on.

RABBI. I've been the rabbi in town for um, now eleven years, I came in 2002. And I came to, uh, Connecticut, uh, particularly Newtown, uh, to live the quiet life. I had been in, um, larger synagogues, where I thought that would make you, meant more success. Bigger synagogue, more success. And you know, just a work horse, cranking out fifty or sixty B'nai Mitzvah ceremonies, you know, um, a year. It's a huge amount of ceremonies to conduct and to educate and prepare and produce. I wasn't at all happy with this. Um, and then the Newtown offering was like a perfect job description. It was small, so small this congregation, small politics...hopefully.

FATHER WEISS. I was under obedience to the bishop when I was the pastor at another parish. I had just finished getting that parish – like we were out of debt, our school was flourishing, and we put up new buildings. And the bishop came to dedicate those buildings.

(Laughs.)

And he said, "You know we're going to need you some other places." It wasn't like two months later when I got a phone call, and I really didn't wanna leave there, it was just like I had it, you know, I thought we had a great place, but he said, "I need you to go to Newtown." So, um, we take a vow of obedience, so when the bishop asks you to do something, I think for the most part, you say yes.

(These next lines should be played as a conversation among the women.)

JENN. Uh, couple of things that I love are, well, first of all, I feel like it's, it's sort of a very intelligent and eclectic mix. There are a lot of people from other areas that moved here. Newtown was written up, years before I was pregnant with my son or had even looked at it, as one of the top ten places to raise kids.

JULIE. A couple of people I worked with, one of them in particular said, "You have to live in Sandy Hook, that's where I lived. It's the best school. It's the best school district! You'll – there's no way you couldn't love it!"

CARRIE. Even just our first experience with the realtor was so nice, and she bent over backwards for us. Um, you know, trying to take us to houses that weren't even on the market yet. She just totally loved living in Sandy Hook. Um, so just even the fact that she loved it so much, um, made a, you know, made a statement.

SALLY. We have probably, I would say we probably have the same memories that any other town has. The Labor Day parade was huge. I marched through the Labor Day parade as a kid down Main Street. It was great. Everybody in town was there. It was fantastic.

CAROLE. Main Street is kind of the site for this, very much out of hand holiday, Halloween tradition. You really have bought the farm if you live on Main Street. I mean, if you bought a house on Main Street, you gotta know what you're in for is all I'm saying. There are so many people, that the candy is donated to the people in these houses to parse out to the thousands of kids that come. Yeah, it is frightening. I kid you not. It is frightening…and not because it's Halloween.

> *(Lights go down on* **SALLY** *and* **CAROLE.** *We hear the opening to "Come, Thou Fount Of Every Blessing" played on the guitar.* **BILL** *steps forward.)*

BILL. On December third, it's usually December third or whatever the first Friday of December is, they have the Christmas tree lighting. And the town of Newtown, all the residents, they put a candle in a bag and they line Main Street. Miles! All up the hill, down the hill, past the pasture and all the way up around the corner. I was driving through and thought, "Wow, My God! This is absolutely breathtaking!" It absolutely takes your breath away. And you know, when you see that, it's forever. You, you, you just don't forget it.

(The **CAST** *starts singing the first verse under the following, as they light candles and congregate together.)*

JULIE. The tree lighting in both Newtown and Sandy Hook doesn't have to be anything spectacular. Uh, it's just a bunch of people crowded around a big tree, but it brings a certain energy that's, uh, that I really haven't found anywhere else.

(Lights down on **JULIE***, as she joins back in with the* **CAST***, who now sing the second verse. After the second verse,* **CARLA** *steps forward.)*

CARLA. It's just quaint, and what you would expect from a small beautiful New England town. It's a very special time here. There was a meteor shower on the thirteenth, and I was standing outside with my two boys that night. We saw seven shooting stars because it's so clear here, and so dark here, you can see all of it. After we went inside and they went to bed, I went outside and made a wish that both my sons would always be safe and happy.

(The **CAST** *blows out their candles, plunging the theater into complete darkness. After a couple of beats, we hear the deafening sound of shattering glass. Lights come up as we hear several different rings of phones receiving calls and/or text messages. Some of the actors answer calls, while others open text messages.)*

My cell phone rang at my desk, and I picked it up as I recognized it as the school. They have, like, an automatic call thing, where you get messages when there's school closings or delays or when something happens. And so it was our superintendent, and all she said was, "All Newtown public schools are in lockdown due to a shooting." Click. And that was it.

DARREN. I'm editing photos that morning and um, I got Photoshop up on a big monitor, and whenever a new email comes in, it flashes briefly in the right hand corner.

This email catches my eye and it says, "The school's in a lockdown, due to a shooting." So I, I, I got up and told Georgia, who was at her desk, "Did you see that message? And as soon as the words came out of my mouth, she turned white... Her worst fear had come true.

JENN. We all thought it was the high school, you know, that's your first instinct, definitely not the elementary school. Um, so I'm sitting there in the hair salon, ya know, I'm sitting there in the chair and starting to panic. One of my babysitters called me and said, "Jenn, I just heard the shooting was on Dickinson Drive, isn't that where Sandy Hook is?"

MIKE. I hear sirens from a distance, like really far out. And we are near the highway, so with no leaves on the trees you do hear, you hear sirens sometimes.

So we were walking back to the office and as I walked back right, right in our property at the Subway there were four teachers. And I intercepted them and I said, "What's going on?" And they were in shock and tears. And they said, "Something very very bad. Gunshots. Many gunshots."

CARRIE. My little one had an ear infection and we had a 9:45 appointment at the doctor's office up the street. The doctor came in late and said, "I'm sorry, all this going on at Sandy Hook."

And then, you know, he kinda examined my daughter and kinda moved on. So we went to the waiting room, in the meantime, and got another phone call that it was, I think they said it was Sandy Hook School. And there were other moms in the waiting room and it really didn't dawn on me what was going on until one of the moms said to me, "It's in the school." Um, and that's when I just kinda thought, "Oh my God." So, um, they just said good luck and I said...

(She gets choked up and pauses.)

"I got two girls in that school."

RABBI. I had a ten o'clock appointment with a Bat Mitzvah girl and her parents. At uh, 10:03, the father, who's a fireman, apologized and said that he had to go, called away from our final rehearsal, as it was the next day. He says, "There's been a shooting at the school."

And so off he goes and we continue our rehearsal. Fifteen minutes later he texts, "This is the worst thing I've ever seen." And then the phone rings and, and it's Father Weiss...Robert Weiss' secretary, and she says...

ACTOR 6. "All clergy go down to the firehouse immediately. All clergy down to the firehouse immediately!"

JENN. By this time there is nothing we can do, the school wasn't answering the phone and everybody was still on lockdown. I was talking to my husband and I got a call – we got a call saying, "You can pick up your kids at the school, at the firehouse." And so I said to my hairdresser, "I gotta go! I gotta get out of here!"

MICHAEL. I told her that I was gonna go to the firehouse and to meet me there.

I didn't want her to know that I knew it was a first grade class, 'cause she couldn't leave where she was and it would make her worry more. So, yeah, I got in my car and I went to the firehouse.

(We hear the sounds of sirens.)

MIKE. It's as if somebody opened the floodgates right in that moment, and every personnel, police, you name it, first responders, in the world was coming. And they came down Church Hill, there really is only one way to come. This is it. I saw the police, and it was a problem because they were coming down this road so fast and this is a bad intersection.

So I'm looking around and I notice none of the police are stopping. So I told my father to keep going, and I went into the road and I was directing traffic for an hour. And as I was doing it, I start to realize this is really significant.

(**MIKE** *starts to direct traffic.*)

CARRIE. I get to Riverside Road and there are just cars all over the place, so I pulled over.

Um, there was a man kinda, you know, telling people where to go and there were just cars parked everywhere.

Um, so I just unrolled the window and I said, "What's going on? Where are the kids?"

MIKE. They're all coming to the firehouse.

CARRIE. So I got my husband on the phone and said, "Come out to the driveway and then I'll pick you up and drop you off as far as I can." So he came out, I dropped him off and he ran down, and I just said "Bring back both of them."

CAROLE. They start combing through the woods or something, and they dragged some guy out and he was like...

ACTOR 2. (*With hands in the air.*) I didn't do anything, I didn't do anything."

CAROLE. Everyone was like, "Oh! They caught one of the gunmen in the woods and they put him in a car –"

ACTOR 2. No! I didn't do anything!

CAROLE. And it was just a neighbor.

(**ACTOR 2** *exits.*)

RABBI. I approached the firehouse and there was a female FBI agent, um, talking to, um, saying, "I want you to go over your class roster. For every name, if there was a person that was absent, then put an X. If there was, um, someone that was present that day, but you know, you saw with your own eyes leave the building, put a check. And if there's somebody that you, third category, that you knew and you saw in school that day but you did not see with your own eyes leaving the building with you or with anybody else, put a circle."

(Lights come up on **JENN**, **JULIE**, *and* **CARRIE**. *Lights out on* **RABBI**.)

JULIE. I was on my way home and in ten minutes I knew my kids were okay 'cause my husband was already there.

(Lights out on **JULIE**.)

CARRIE. My husband called a few minutes later and said he found one daughter and he's gonna go look for the other. And then he called me back and said he got them both.

(Lights out on **CARRIE**. *Only* **JENN** *is still in light.)*

JENN. I, I just can't even describe how panicked it started to get for me because he wasn't answering his phone and the texts were flying. "Okay, do you have him?" "Why aren't you answering me?" "Where's our son?" "What's going on?"

And I was just leaving him these messages and starting to get that rising panic inside, like something's not right because he's avoiding me.

DARREN. Then they said there was no second shooter and the shooter inside was dead. Um, and they said, they uh, he was –

(Sniffles.)

He was found dead in a classroom, found in a classroom.

And at that point I, uh, I broke down. I mean, I went out into the yard and just picked up the first stick I could find and just beat the fuck out of a tree, because I knew that was the worst case, shoo-shoo-shooter killing himself. I-I knew he didn't just walk in and shoot himself in front of the kids. And I –

(Sniffles.)

Couldn't imagine –

(His voice breaks with emotion.)

Why? I knew with that, you know, the information, there was more than the three –

(Sniffles.)

Him being in a classroom. And the numbers, we just watched in horror, as it went from a handful...to a dozen...twenty.

(Beat.)

And I thought, we've topped Columbine.

RABBI. The female, blondish FBI agent that was most in charge in the room, started coming our way. And I, um, said, "I'm going to talk to this lady," and I say, "Look, I'm Rabbi Praver, I know what's happened, now what can I do to help?" And she said, "Come with me," and then we walked through a corridor to the back room.

(We see **JENN** *in the background, looking at her phone in very dim lighting.)*

MICHAEL. When I got there it was pretty, they'd taken all the fire trucks out, so it was fully empty, all the bays, um, and there weren't many people there. There were a few parents and a few, um, teacher aides were there, and they were holding signs for the different classes to line up. And you know, it was almost maybe ten minutes and the kids started pouring into the firehouse and they were all sort of lining up by their, um, by their number.

More and more kids were coming in and I didn't see his teacher, I didn't see any of his classmates, I didn't see him and I went from one end of the firehouse to the other.

I saw his teacher and so I started moving over to where she was, and she was walking, she had four or five kids, you know in each, they were all holding hands but none of them were him, and then my heart dropped.

(We see **MICHAEL** *looking around.)*

JENN. So, he finally calls me and says...

MICHAEL. I have him.

JENN. And I just went like,
"Okayyyy."

(She breathes out a huge sigh of relief.)

MICHAEL. And I went over and gave him a big hug, and I mean, they were all still in a state of shock. And then we signed, I signed for release, um, and on the way out he wanted a drink of water. I don't have any water on me, so he said "Oh no, there's water in the back."

All the kids were coming through in through the, um, back door of the firehouse and I guess there were drinks back there.

RABBI. And so, uh, this is the back room for the families that got the circle on that roster.

MICHAEL. It was a small room with couches, two couches, and like a bar with little Dixie cups of water on it.

So he got a drink and then we saw, so in the room was one of our friends and she's like, "Have you seen my son?" Her son is a first-grader also and one of our son's close friends.

I told her we hadn't and that I'd stay until her husband got there. So we're there consoling her as best I could, you know, "He's a good kid, it's gonna be fine. His class was late, they just got up here and I'm sure his class will be coming soon."

RABBI. I walked around and uh, it didn't take more than fifteen seconds before I saw Veronique and Lenny Posner.

Veronique is sitting there glassy-eyed and saying to me, "Rabbi, I don't know what I, I can't go on if, if Noah is dead. I... I just can't go on. I just can't...no, no no! That would be too much!"

MICHAEL. So then her husband comes and then he leaves to go, to go um, look for their sons and I say, "You sure you don't want me to stay? You know I'll stay."

"No, no you guys should go. My husband's here and he'll be back in a minute."

And so then, you know, we left and by that time the firehouse was almost empty. Almost all the kids had been matched up with their parents.

CAROLE. The governor was there, Pat was there and we had accounted for the children. All the children. We had to account for 600 children. So everybody was involved in this decision, which was we were waiting for, ya know, for the police to do their thing and um –

(Smacks lips.)

Coroners were coming in and um, the EMTs were there. And, um, they knew, you know, what this was going to be. And the governor took it upon himself, he said, "I can't. I had to make the decision." And he went into the back room of the firehouse, and well, let them know. They weren't coming out.

RABBI. People were falling on the floor, crying, tearing their hair out and then they spread... They were spreading out.

After the announcement came there was a rapid fire of clergy, and that was something that was very powerful for me. This was the – this was real. This was real religion.

One guy starts to pray and he says his prayer and he's done. Then another guy gets up and he says his prayer, like a rapid fire, you know? And it's just a scene of tragedy, of a national scale mega tragedy, and these are the last rites or the last, you know, utterances of the spirit. Our different houses of worship there delivering it up.

CAROLE. The safety of this little town, it's like when Kennedy died, that peace overall has been shattered. I think that's the biggest thing that happened here, the shattering of the illusion of...our little world.

How did this happen to us? And the magnitude of every flag in the nation at half-staff for Newtown. What? What just happened here?

> *(We hear an acoustic mournful version of "Come Thou Fount" play as the* **CAST** *walks over to the chalkboards and writes the names of the victims.* **YOLIE** *tries to make sense of what just happened.)*

YOLIE. Twenty-six pebbles. That's exactly what happened. Each one of those drop in a pond, and you know, it just emanates out. The ripples, the vibrations... It's life. This stuff spreads.

> *(The* **CAST** *begins to try to console one other, but just before any physical connection is made, a floodlight pops up on them [or the flash of a camera].)*

> *(***Projection:*** *Clips from news reports* on Newtown begin to project onto the wall chalkboards, which now act as small televisions. This builds into a cacophony of noise.)*

FATHER. I just got swarmed. I mean, I was literally swarmed. And I couldn't get out. And I will say there were, at that point, there was so much confusion and so much goss— um, rumor, and I wasn't the great clarifier. I'm just, I just know what I went through inside the room, you know? Don't get me wrong, I think the story needs to be out there and I think it needs to continue to be out there. But I'd never seen anything like it in my life. I

---

*Licensees may not use clips from actual publications of any kind, but must create the projected clips themselves, in the style of headlines that appeared after the shooting.

mean there were literally hundreds and hundreds there in just the first few hours.

CAROLE. Horrible. Invasive. It was like a rape. There was no escape and there was no time for us to grieve. We would all be watching everybody and when somebody went down... I mean at the grocery store people would, would go down to their knees and there was a hive of people that would be there to just let them cry. You know? And you can't, you can't do that with the media because it's so intrusive. They just want – man they want you sobbing. They want to see you in pain. We had to actually put up signs on the doors of town hall that said, "No Press!"

CARRIE. The next day we printed out the list of names and we brought the kids into the TV room and said, "We found out who was hurt, um, and some people died, some teachers died." And we told them first, we said that "Dawn Hochsprung – Mrs. Hochsprung is gone. She didn't make it."

They immediately started crying 'cause my older daughter just loved her so much. Um, she started crying and my first-grader just, just put her hands over her ears and said, "I don't wanna hear anymore."

JENN. I went to a counseling center and said to them, "How am I supposed to tell my son this? Please tell me how?" And I asked them, "Guys can I workshop this with you a little?" They said they couldn't and then I was just basically in shock.

So I asked, "Well can we just write this down because I don't know what you just said to me?" So I wrote it down and we sat down with our son and we told him the next day, ya know, who um, and then...that his best friend was gone.

DARREN. The whole intersection just wall-to-wall satellite trucks, ya know, ya know? Dishes everywhere. You can't see the buildings from the dishes.

GEORGIA. Yeah, it's just. And you're just thinking, why? There's this – the press never comes to Newtown for anything, I mean...

DARREN. We have our local newspaper the *Newtown Bee* and it takes a week to generate enough local news. "We're having a bake sale!"

GEORGIA. And, like my first reaction was kind of weird. I kinda felt comforted by it in some kinda weird way. It was like, ya know, it was like the world recognizing that this was the most horrendous thing that's happened on the face of the Earth, ya know? In my opinion. And kind of bearing witness to that and saying, "Wow, this is so big we have to be here."

DARREN. There's no place, ya-ya-ya-you're immune to it. There's no place within Newtown or Sandy Hook that you could go. Um, it took us to get from our house to Sandy Hook normally, maybe five minutes. The first couple of weeks you'd have to allow at least an hour to get, to get into town because of the traffic jams. People, ya know, every news truck, every pe-people, ya know, because the highway sign says "Newtown," people pull off the highway just to see. Just to see.

(**YOLIE** *walks in carrying a rolled-up poster.*)

YOLIE. I felt, well maybe I could absorb some of this sadness or maybe I could deflect some of this by just standing in this like, vigil. Sort of like silent vigil. I woke up and thought, "Oh my God, if this is what my town is now known for, I just couldn't bear it." And what was this? I was compelled and I had this dream and I said, I woke up and I said, "I have to go make a sign. I have to go make a sign and go sit out somewhere."

So I called my friend Vicky and said to her, "I'm gonna make a sign and it's gonna say 'I am love, I am Newtown' and I'm gonna sit at the highway exit. Exit ten. So that it's the first thing they see when they come in and the last thing they see when they leave. So, me and my daughter, made this sign.

(**YOLIE** *unrolls the poster board and displays the sign and sits on the map between the flagpole and Sandy Hook.*)

MIKE. Well everybody was up in arms and I said, "Listen, listen, this is the center of the world right now. Think about it. Sandy Hook is the center of the world...the universe...it's here."

I knew that without them here, the rest of the world wouldn't be able to get all of the details. Wouldn't be able to mourn with us. They're doing their job and they were respectful.

YOLIE. I sat there for like hours, and everyone would come up, and all the media, and I was just like, "Don't ask me a thing I am in silent vigil and just holding this space. This is my message and no you cannot have my name." And I just sat there and I did this because...we are this.

MIKE. There are only so many places to go in Sandy Hook and that's what I told everybody. Where do you want them to go? Where do you want them to park? Explain it to me. Can't go to the schools. Can't go to the firehouse. The park is jammed. The park – I don't know if you've been to – you couldn't park there. Where could they go? Where could those people go? You have to be rational about it. People here are sick, they're crying too. I had news reporters crying. They said, "I've never cried before." They'd been to wars. And when I saw them emotional, I knew we're all in this together. The whole country is in this together. What are you going to do?

JENN. The next week was just funerals and wakes and – it was – it was pretty indescribable.

(*We see and hear flashes of media cameras.*)

MICHAEL. Please! Just, just let us mourn.

(*The* **CAST** *forms a straight line down "Main Street" as if they are waiting in line with* **JOE** *at the end.*)

JOE. I stood in line for the principal's funeral and had to miss class. Here I am thinking, "It's a town away, I'm going to go pay my respects."

I had a card I had prepared, um, to leave for the family, a-a-a note I had written, and I got there a bit late. There were news cameras, that weren't allowed to be up close, and lots of police, and the line went out the building, around the block, down the corner and we're talking about, like, rural blocks. You know, like, a mile, there's a mile-long line easily. So I went to the end of the line and I stood there with my hands in my pockets freezing my ass off and I wouldn't leave.

I'm just standing there looking at the flag. They had put, it was like really iconic, they had dropped a gigantic American flag from a boom arm of a fire truck right over the road, right before the whole crowd would walk in to pay their respects to them. And it was a really strong gathering moment. Everybody was there because she represented what was wonderful about that school.

And...

(Beat.)

I don't know man...

(Beat.)

It's – that was tough, that was really tough. And I was in and out in less than five minutes and waited in line for more than four hours. But I shook her husband's hand, and there was uh, you know, lots of sadness. There's no way to – no other way to put it.

(The stage goes into darkness again and we hear a portion of President Obama's speech at the Newtown Vigil. During this speech, we see **JENN** *write "Winter" on the wall chalkboards.)*

PRESIDENT OBAMA'S SPEECH. *(Pre-recorded.)* "...And that's what should drive us forward in everything we do, for as long as God sees fit to keep us on this Earth.

God has called them all home. For those of us who
remain, let us find the strength to carry on, and make
our country worthy of their memory."

JENN. I don't know. I still can't explain why something like
this would happen. I just think of the brutality of it,
and I think, how could any God let something like that
happen?

FATHER WEISS. I really have been put into a very different
role than I ever expected. Well you know now... I've...
I'm like the leader of the community and I don't see
myself in that role, you know? I saw myself as a pastor
of St. Rose and that's what you do. That's the way I
understand it, that's what priests do. And, you know,
so now I have this, I can never decide if it's ascribed
or achieved leadership. It's put a lot of pressure on me,
um, that I normally wouldn't put on myself, you know?
I'll be honest, I've kept my distance from the families
because I'm a mess personally. We had eight of the
funerals here, and um, it...it still gets to me. I just
can't talk with them. We're very present with them, we
have staff doing everything they can to support and
encourage them, but I just have to keep my distance
from them right now.

KAT. It was just evil. It was just evil, there was no reasoning,
ya know? A soul was lost and took others with him,
ones that didn't deserve to go. My spiritual belief is
though that they will be back, just different names,
different families, different everything, so there'll be
another soul coming back through.

Um, I think I did pray more to Gaia, you know Mother
Earth, and was real taken aback that she would take
that many young souls, uh...at one moment.

I know there's evil on this earth and sadly it's found
its way to our town and I just asked her to bring those
souls back quickly, ya know?

STARR. Does this shake my faith? No.

JERIANN. No.

STARR. Absolutely no, it actually makes us stronger.

JERIANN. Yeah. Stronger.

STARR. And us both, th-that's why we're here, to help not just those...but everybody.

(*They begin to hand out business cards again.*)

JERIANN. Anybody that needs help, yeah.

STARR. And it actually built us both I guess.

JERIANN. Yeah, made us stronger. Um, just healing-wise for me, I mean, I'm always healing myself, but healing other people.

STARR. Yeah, I mean I've seen her go, like if someone's in the store and someone has uh...we had um...

JERIANN. I had five in one day. Right in a row. And then I think I took maybe a five or ten minute break just to get some water. And after that I was almost ready to pass out.

STARR. How about the reporters?

JERIANN. Yeah.

STARR. I was doing a news, um...

JERIANN. A filming.

STARR. A filming! And I said, "Jer! These reporters need help!" She didn't even hesitate. She just –

(*Makes a "whooshing" sound.*)

Right to it. She – she shielded them, ya know, tried to... ya know, ya know... We're hoping for the best.

CARLA. I don't know if you believe any of this stuff, but you seem to be open-minded, so, uh, I heard from one of the kids that died. Jesse Lewis. I told a friend and he said to me, "You gotta talk to Scarlett, you gotta talk to Scarlett Lewis." So I asked him to ask her if she would let me do a free healing on her. I didn't want to say, "I just heard from your son," you know? So we became closer and I channeled her son for her. If I wasn't able to communicate with Jesse, you know what I mean, I think that... I don't... I think I'd be a real mess. I think that the way I felt from Jesse's side was he's very strong and he actually told – he and his mother both knew he wasn't going to live very long.

And before he died, I can show inside, I'll show you inside, he drew on his chalkboard three words, "Healing," "Nurturing" and "Love."

He drew this on his chalkboard and he's like six, you know? And when I connect with him, he's very strong, he feels like a general. And he saved like ten kids' lives during the shooting, when the gun jammed, he was like, "Go, go, go! The gun jammed!"

He's six years old! And he got these kids running, and they're all in shock and if he hadn't said that, they'd be standing there. There'd be ten more bodies. And I think he was already shot at the time and he still said that, and ummm...he's so, so strong. And he's so amazing. So maybe I need that, maybe that helps me keep faith.

RABBI. This was not an act of God, this was an act of man. Um, you got free will and so that means that anything could happen. Adolf Hitler can happen. Senseless deaths and shootouts and hold-ups and robberies can happen and do happen every day in this country.

CARRIE. The thing was, people kept telling me, "Well, God gave you free will. He did this, it wasn't God's doing. It was his free will. He chose to do this." But I guess my questions are, well, if he had a mental illness then it isn't really free will. He can't help it right?

Then my daughter asks me, "Is he in hell?" And we tried to explain, "Well you know, he was probably sick and he didn't know what he was doing." And then she would ask, "Well if he was sick then that means he wasn't an evil person, so would God forgive him? What if he's sorry? Does he still have to go to hell?" These are questions that we as adults don't have the answer for.

(**CARRIE** *turns and faces the rest of the cast.*)

What does a parent do?

(The cast drops all character and delivers the following lines straight to the audience.)

ACTOR 2. In the shooter's home, police found the following.

ACTOR 3. A seven-foot pole, with a blade on one side and a spear on the other.

ACTOR 4. A metal bayonet.

ACTOR 5. Three samurai swords.

ACTOR 6. .323 caliber bolt-action rifle.

ACTOR 1. .22 caliber Savage Mark II rifle

ACTOR 2. .22 Volcanic starter pistol

ACTOR 3. News articles on the 2008 shooting at Northern Illinois University.

ACTOR 6. And inside his gun safe was a holiday card from his mother, containing a check for the purchase of his next firearm.

*(**JENN** writes "The Boy" on the wall chalkboards.)*

JENN. Well, ya know, of course I'm – I'm angry. I'm angry at his mother especially and I'm angry at his father and his brother, because obviously there was a lot more to this story in terms of his upbringing and his... Just the lack of care that he probably received as a child and all that. And I also blame her friends because did anybody not see this woman wasn't all together? And did nobody say anything? And what about her ex-husband? Didn't he ever go to the house and see these guns?

KAT. Um, I think he's someone who fell through the cracks somehow. And it happens. You don't always notice the –

(Long pause.)

I have a person that I knew that kind of, you know, fell through the cracks and, uh, eventually as time went on he ended up committing suicide. How do you know that you know when a person truly needs...the support that they need?

(Pause.)

KAT. This was actually my first husband.

I even... I well... I knew he had problems, but I didn't know how deep the problem was and I divorced him. So where do you...? It's just sadly some people fall through the cracks and you don't even know it.

JOE. What...what did he teach us in that evil act? That we're not safe? That's what he was trying to teach. That's what he was trying to do. That's not the lesson we should take from it, you know? And everybody knows that, but they can't help but feel a little less safe.

GEORGIA. Not that I'm blaming, ya know, not that I'm pointing fingers or blaming any one person, but the village raises the child. I think one of the biggest problems was his isolation.

Humans are not meant to be in isolation, ya know, we're meant to be connected. And when someone's not connected...bad things start to happen.

STARR. I did know him, and honestly, a lot of his family. He was, um, he was a good kid, but unfortunately even though it was a "huggy town," kids from about, um, sixth grade up to eighth grade form a click.

DARREN. Our son came to us and said, "I feel bad. I-I feel guilty."

About what?

He said, "I should have said something."

What do you mean you should have said something? I mean, my heart's starting to pound.

And, um, he said, "Well, when we had the Halloween party, all the kids and me were sitting around and talking about how he was really weird."

And I asked him, well, weird how?

"Oh just, just weird."

And I said, well was that it?

"Well basically."

So, I mean, it's nothing to be ashamed of. Look, there are a lot of weird people, we can't report them for being weird.

MIKE. Yeah, what do you do? Start incarcerating people because they look funny? Then it's not America anymore.

STARR. He kind of got pushed to the side and I think his mom did what she had to do.

DARREN. I think even when he was in high school, that he would kind of walk with his back against the wall down the lockers to go from class to class. That kind of stuff gets the attention of other kids, um, that's just a fact of life that we all know.

Um, we've all been through some type of incident growing up, where someone has pointed out that you're different for whatever reason.

STARR. His mother, father and him had counseling just before the divorce.

Three months prior to this incident, he was fine, then he was disturbed that it was a final decision that Dad moved and brother moved. He had nobody else to talk to. And that just...snapped the camel's back.

When he was on medication and in therapy, he was the one who would take his shirt off...off his...off his back to help you. He was the one that, uh, did tutoring for the younger. He was the one who would, like uh, scold the younger if he found him smoking pot. So, ya know, they forgot about these good things about him.

FATHER WEISS. I always have twenty-eight candles out. I believe in forgiveness. And that is one of the big issues. Is it twenty-six or twenty-eight? A very sensitive issue.

> (**JENN** *becomes enraged at this and leaves the* *stage.* **GEORGIA** *and* **MIKE** *follow her with a* *"Wait!")*

SALLY. I'll be happy to talk about this. You're talking to a family that actually has somebody with a pretty serious mental illness. My brother is schizophrenic and there was a good five years –

BILL & CAROLE. Ten years.

SALLY. Ten years that was grey. Grey as could be. No black, no white. What is he gonna do? I have no idea what my brother is gonna do.

CAROLE. The thing is, and maybe it's not appropriate, but twenty-eight people died that day. It wasn't twenty-six, it was twenty-eight people who lost their lives. Twenty-eight families that mourned.

SALLY. I think that his mother did everything she possibly could. There is a point where you are scared, you're afraid, but it's your son. And you have hope because he's not a monster, he's mentally ill. He doesn't think like the rest of us. It's like what you said Dad, "Some people honestly just don't know the difference between right and wrong."

BILL. A very good friend of mine explained it perfectly. He said, "There is no difference between a man who's being chased by someone with a machine gun, and a man who THINKS he's being chased by someone with a machine gun."

Our parents teach us things and it sticks with us and then we pass it on to our children. Then there's this little hiccup where everything you taught them just goes away. And you just sit there and think, "Who stole my son away from me?" And the sad part is that he was over eighteen years old, and legally there's not a thing we could do. We're no different from Mrs. Lanza, because we let our son function also and there wasn't a thing we could do about it.

RABBI. Adam was a gifted child that we failed. I gotta believe that if there was someone there – big brother – highly trained, that could sit him down eyeball to eyeball and say, "Listen Adam, you are different and a lot of kids said that you're strange, but that's because you're different. I want to introduce you to some people that are like you, that have Asperger's and are researchers and actuaries or different things that have intense mathematics involved. You can be in the forefront of medical research with your skills. Very few people can do that. You've got it. And I wanna help. I'm gonna help you find your way in this life, in this world, because you're gifted. And some people will call you strange...or...or...or bully you for that. I know that we all get bullied. Join, you know, join the club. You're in the club. But, I'm your friend and I'll be meeting with you every week. Some days we'll go out and play, shoot some hoops, and some days we're gonna go out and just talk. We're mammals, we flock together. We need to be together."

CAROLE. One of the things that really struck during all this, was when I heard that Adam's body wasn't being claimed. That was a week's worth of staying up at night.

JOE. The only thing any asshole does, is that he succeeds in becoming infamous. And...and he will become a mark in a history book, in some cases, if we let him. What do you do? How do you bury people like that so people forget them? Because that's what you need to do. You need to forget them.

CARLA. I think we're all trying to find our place now. I knew who I was before December fourteenth, and now it's like, "Who am I? What am I supposed to do? How do I help? What can I do?" Then you just feel like you're adding to the noise.

CARRIE. Well, for... I think for many, many moms, we have become, um, accidental activists. If you can call it that. For me, at that first meeting with the psychologist, I said to her, "I just don't know what to do. I really don't. I'm so angry at this gun stuff. I just don't know what to do." And she said, "Well you can't focus on what has happened. If you're really angry about the gun stuff, focus on that." So that was actually a good idea. So after that meeting, I just started sending emails to my legislate – like, the Connecticut, um, all the lawmakers. Whoever I could get an email address to, whoever's website I could go to and click, and I would just free-form type. I was just so mad and so upset at the gun stuff, because I never really, um, knew about it before. I'm not really... I was never really pro-gun, but I wasn't really anti-gun. And now, it's like, your eyes are just open to this stuff and now you just can't close 'em.

> (*As the* **RABBI** *speaks, the rest of the* **CAST**, *with the exception of* **CARLA**, *goes toward him to hear this speech.*)

RABBI. Newtown doesn't want to be remembered as the town of the tragedy. We want to be remembered as the bridge to a new and kinder world. It's not about the suburbs or the urban area. It's not about the rural areas. It's about the red blood that flows out of all of our veins. It's about the clear tears that flow out of our eyes. We are all the same...

CARLA. There were these people demonstrating outside the NSSF building, which is on the corner. And this building, I don't think anyone knew what it was before, it's National Shooting, it's like sports recreational shooting. So they're a resource for people who hunt and so they're a resource to let people know where they're able to hunt and shoot and what the rules are. And it's a very positive organization, and it's been here for decades. So yeah, people were outside it saying, "Get out of Newtown! Get out! Get out!"

> (*The cast start chanting "Get Out" with a hushed intensity under this next section.* **ACTOR 2** *holds a sign up that says "Get Out!")*

And, I went in the grocery store after passing by them and seeing the signs, and I just start bawling. Bawling, bawling and bawling. I'm like, stop crying you're in the grocery store, I'll cry in the car. Please stop. And I just had to check out with all my crap like that, crying through the whole process, and it was like, "Aw, man..." you know? That sucked.

*(The **RABBI** is now at a fever pitch leading this protest.)*

RABBI. We live in a society of 32,000 deaths by guns alone every year! If these people died in the battlefields of Afghanistan, we wouldn't accept it. Yet when it happens right here in the cities of America, we somehow are mysteriously silent!

CARLA. And now I'm crying in the car, I couldn't even drive, so I pull over to the demonstrators and say, "You guys! Stop the hatefulness! You're part of the hate!"

ACTOR 2. This isn't hate, this is love!

CARLA. "That makes me even more sad, you think this is love? There's a sign that says *Get Out*, that's not hate?"

ACTOR 2. *(Looking at his sign.)* "Well, okay that's hate."

CARLA. I was just begging, begging for them to stop, stop making – stop perpetuating this hate. There's so much division now, and it's very strange 'cause it's like *(Snaps fingers.)* overnight.

FATHER WEISS. You get, uh, so desensitized to it. You know, to just violence as a way of life today. This really kind of dark side or this cultural death, or whatever you want to call it, it is just – it's overwhelming us.

MIKE. That's not the problem. We have no social skills in America anymore. The parents want us to teach their kids to be verbal and vocalized and they have a hard time. I played outside all my life. My parents gave me a Nintendo and it came with three games. You remember that? Donkey Kong, Mario Brothers and I want to say Zelda. It was stupid. It was terrible. That was it. That's all we had. I wanted something else and they said, "That's what you get." And after a while you say, "Forget this." And then you wanted to go outside. We just don't have social skills.

FATHER WEISS. And when someone's not connected…bad things start to happen.

There's gonna be trauma.

(We hear the same crash of glass that we heard earlier in the play.)

JULIE. My son's teacher, Ms. Roig, was fast and furious.

CARRIE. She's my hero.

JULIE. She had them in a morning meeting, quiet, and she heard the noise blowing through the doors and windows and she instantly just said, "Bathroom."

JENN. And she got them all in the bathroom within the room and closed the door, and I think she pulled a sort of a little bookcase in front of the door of the bathroom.

JULIE. It was literally seconds because he had to have walked by her room to get to Vicky Soto's room. And so they sat in the bathroom listening to everything for however long it was. My son was trying to talk her into running, you know, "We can get out of here," he said, "I don't wanna die. I don't wanna miss Christmas."

CARRIE. My daughter said that one of the scariest parts was when the police came, because they knocked on the door and they didn't know if it was the bad guy. She truly thought she was going to die and that the bad guy, or bad guys were coming in.

Ms. Roig didn't open the door and made the police slide their badge under the door before she would open it. My husband talked to her when he was at the firehouse and she said to him, "There's gonna be trauma."

JENN. "There's gonna be trauma."

JULIE. "They heard everything."

*(**JENN** writes, "The Monsters" on the wall chalkboard.)*

They seem to be okay for a while, then my son started to show signs of Post Traumatic Stress Disorder, PTSD, maybe within a week after. So then, we as a family went just into, "How do we make it better for him," um, and we didn't know how.

CARRIE. The first grade class and whoever was, like, in that hallway, in that area, and they're – they are completely different because they actually thought they were dying that day.

JULIE. It was noises, it was locking all the doors, he needed to make sure all the doors were locked. He would walk around the house, he would hear the garage door open and was afraid that somebody was coming into our house.

CARRIE. She wouldn't leave my side or my husband's side or a grown-up's side. She was taking... We were giving her melatonin almost every night to help her fall asleep because her teachers would tell me she would have her head on her desk during class. She had huge bags under her eyes.

JENN. I guess with PTSD you just have that fear of not being safe. So kids, children, end up just being scared. They weren't scared of monsters before? Now they're scared of monsters.

CARRIE. So now she's scared of werewolves. She's scared of, um, bombs. She's afraid of bombs. She thinks somebody's putting a bomb in our house. At the time somebody was working on our generator and she's asking, "Is he putting a bomb in the generator? What is he doing? Why is he in our house?"

DARREN. We don't know all the things that are broken, we're still discovering them, 'cause we've been asleep and haven't been paying attention. I've read a lot about Columbine, ya know, ten to fourteen years later on. The principal, um, said he, ya know, he's had kids go through that were fine. They appeared to be fine, went to college, ya know, appeared to be fine, got married, appeared to be fine, had children and bam! They just fell to pieces. Generational PTSD. With our society, it's – it's a sense of, ya know, a – a bit of shame. Especially for younger people to say, and now that's why I came out and said, "Look, yes, I've got PTSD!" I'm thinking of having a T-shirt made, ya know, "Got PTSD? I do."

JENN. People here are afraid. You know? It's scary to talk about it because you don't know who's been touched by what. There are times I want to drive away and never come back, and then there are times when I never want to leave. I just think it's all... Everyone is so afraid. And that's what it is. If I get really mad, I'm not gonna crumble into a puddle, which is what I really need and want to do, because if I let myself go there, what's gonna happen to me? I don't know if I'll ever recover. How could you possibly... How do you process all of this?

CAROLE. This – this is what happened to us, because so much happened that we weren't allowed a moment to really grieve for these babies.

But I remember the morning the flags went back up, because I had heard about it, and I drove in – I was getting there at some, at some crazy hour in the morning. I called David on the phone, my guy who helps me with the building, and I said, "Get over here and get that flag up! I want the big flag up in the center of town. Raise those flags, get 'em back up where they're supposed to be!" And then we just watched. David raised the flags back up and I thought, "Okay, alright, we're getting our town back. Now all you people leave!"

(Laughs.)

(The lights fade, and we hear the sounds of large cargo trucks pulling up. During this, **JENN** *writes, "The Flood" on the wall chalkboards. The* **CAST** *then walks onstage with boxes full of brightly-colored cards, teddy bears, and letters, pouring the contents all over the stage floor. They exit, and as light comes up on* **CHRIS,** *they re-enter with empty boxes and start sorting the mail.)*

CHRIS. I'm Chris. Um, and I guess what you're looking for is, um, shortly after the fourteenth I was put in charge of logistics of all the "in-town" relations, uh, which is what they were called. I was in charge of everything that came in, um, how to handle it, how to bring it in and then eventually disbursement. So, I kind of ran that show, I had a lot of help, but I was put in charge of it.

BILL. Well I wanna tell you something, doing the mail is tough.

CAROLE. I know it is.

BILL. Doing the mail is tough, you know, and you had to – the only way you could really do it successfully was just block yourself. Just block yourself and just do it.

CAROLE. I know, but it was such a healing for so many people.

CHRIS. Facebook being the wonderful thing that it is, um, somebody decided it would be a wonderful idea to start sending to – to, uh, send teddy bears to Newtown. And I had seen it in the news and I didn't think much of it. By Monday morning she had brought in a couple of bags, my girlfriend, 'cause they were, they were giving teddy bears and toys and stuff across the way. She says, "If I could get more that would be great," so we went to the church and they had a fourth grade classroom full...to my waist! And you're as big as I am.

(Points to a member of the audience.)

It was just, it was just a full fourth grade classroom with thousands of bears in that one room alone, that was just over that first weekend. So, um, that opened my eyes a little bit as to what the scale was going to be like.

CARLA. It ended up being so strange that everywhere we went my son kept getting free teddy bears...free!

People...the whole world, was like pouring all this love on us, you know? And there was such amazing love just pouring in from everywhere. And it, and then you start to think, like, that was twenty kids lost all at the same time. It was horrific, it was a massacre, it was a tragedy. Then you think how many kids die in Chicago every year to probably pretty poor moms. You know what I mean? And how they grow up with this violence and then nobody does anything for those parents.

CHRIS. I started putting up signs and I take a phone call, it was Dennis from ACE Trailer, he says, "Oh you know, I can drop off some trailers. What do you need?" I said, "Drop off whatever you can, 'cause we're gonna start running out of room," and we filled those trailers by Thursday. People were driving in, we had people from Nebraska, Florida, um, Iowa, Texas. People drove from Texas to drop off teddy bears!

BILL. And the hugs! This class in Africa made these silhouettes of their bodies giving a hug.

SALLY. With their face!

CAROLE. *(Extends arms far apart.)* It was this big!

BILL. And the arms go out too... It's just... It's the cutest.

CAROLE. And we hung them up on the wall and anytime anybody was starting to get, well, really down doing the mail we'd say, "Go get a hug!"

KAT. "You need help? I'm here!" And that's how it started. I help friends all the time, so I thought about it and says, "You know, these people are just friends I haven't met yet and oh boy do they need help."

CHRIS. People needed to do it for themselves, and that's what a lot of it turned out to be. Newtown is not a poor community, ya know? There are some pockets of... some pockets of broke, but there's no real poverty like in other towns.

So we didn't really need 63,700 teddy bears.

CAROLE. Everybody's on edge, everybody's looking, everybody's watching, everybody's scared...and it's not us! Its, it's the world, which is what we've been trying to get across to people who call that wanna send another 60,000 teddy bears. You need to look at your own children. They're scared, they need counseling, they need teddy bears. Do it there. We're...we're... We got 'em. We got the teddy bears. Trust me. Give 'em to your children in honor of ours.

KAT. The other problem was the overwhelming number of volunteers. Way too many, way too many and they would, you know, you'd have a hundred people that show up one day, you train all of them and then tomorrow was another different hundred and then you had to train them. So it was chaos.

The hard part was the families would come to the warehouse and pick up their items. I didn't know any of them at first, but I kept my, uh, title going by just going up to them. "Hey, how ya doing? I'm Kat, if you need anything," and you know, they'd put out their hand and I say, "No, no, no, I give hugs."

CHRIS. So we wound up sending stuff all over. First we gave the families their options on where they wanted stuff to go. So if families wanted stuff to go to "Green Chimneys," we'd send stuff to "Green Chimneys." Or if they wanted their stuff to go to, um, Lakota Indians, I managed to send a tractor-trailer-worth of stuff to the Lakota Indian tribe for free.

We sent a lot of stuff down to Hurricane Sandy. I sent stuff to a mission in India, where the kids don't have much. I had stuff go to Kenya, I had stuff go to Haiti, a lot of police stations so they can keep teddy bears in their trunks again. We took care of all the battered women shelters, um, hospitals, the toy closets and stuff for all the children's hospitals. I mean, I have a list of them if you wanna see it, of where stuff went, but everywhere was somewhere good. I got to do it all for – had to do it all for free. We didn't have a budget for any of it...so, for free. It was done on the backs of volunteers.

YOLIE. The ripples, the vibrations... This stuff spreads.

CAROLE. Then we had Yolie.

BILL. I've been hearing about Yolie, for what, six months now? Five months now anyway. She keeps saying, "What kind of a name is Yolie?"

> (**YOLIE** *begins to spread out some of the cards and photograph them in the corner.*)

CAROLE. We were, well, now I hope I'm telling the right story, we were obviously very in it. We were in the hallways of town hall, and we had decided that, uh, we were going to display everything that came in. So we get the tables out into the hallway, and get the tablecloths out and such and put it all in the mail bins. Then there's this skinny little rump kid and she's out in the hallway and she's going up and down and she's going through all the cards and she's sort of settled in and I didn't know who she was. She had a camera and she's taking pictures.

> *(To **YOLIE**.)*

Hi, What are you doing?

YOLIE. I'm just taking pictures.

CAROLE. What do you mean you're just taking pictures? You've been taking pictures of hundreds of thousands of cards?

> *(Back to the audience.)*

So the next day I went out there, and there she was, the cards are now fanned out and she's getting – creeping into new territory. She's out there and she's making a mess on my table!

> *(To **YOLIE**.)*

What are you doing?

YOLIE. Well, I'm not doing anything, I just wanted to kinda get...

> *(Makes a fanned out gesture with her hands.)*

CAROLE. Then I went back the next day and the cards are on the floor and they're spread out all over the place.

> *(To **YOLIE**.)*

Okay, we're going to have to have a talk here. What is it you want to do?

> *(**YOLIE**'s response starts off toward **CAROLE** and then to the audience.)*

YOLIE. My mission is to have an online collection that represents all of this. So that anyone who has lost their children, or brothers, or sisters, or aunts, uncles, whatever, they can look at these and be like, "Wow, that really helps! Wow, that really, really helps!" They can print out the stuff and make a book for themselves. There are, you know, poems that people have written and just be like – it just makes you feel good. It can be as simple as someone wrote on a big piece of paper and it just said "No Words, love Trey," a mother of two in Texas, and you're like, "Oh yeah, that's it."

CAROLE. I think she's nuts for doing this, but she's doing this.

BILL. She turned from being just someone who walked in there and she's now –

CAROLE. Now she's got the keys to the kingdom. She can do whatever she wants to.

YOLIE. Do you know the idea of Agape? It's like, just loving people because they deserve it. And I don't love, well I guess I can say, love everyone. You don't have to like everyone, you don't have to live with them, you don't have to be friends with them, but you have to build a community where everyone has...where there's something for everyone. And so, the connections that are being made and what we're really trying to do is to make this a model for what we're supposed to be doing from now on.

> *(The* **CAST** *has finished sorting the mail and walks the boxes off. We hear the sound of a school bell ringing and* **JENN** *writes "Spring" on the wall chalkboards.)*

CARRIE. My daughter finally went back to school and they had no help in the room whatsoever. No trauma people in the room. No doctors. Nothing. They had these, like, special helpers, which didn't really help the kids.
When a child had an issue, um, in the classroom, it was the special helper's job to kinda take the child out of

the classroom, go read a book, kinda just redirect them, get them in a happier place and then return back to the classroom.

So, they had that, but that really wasn't doing anything. Every time I had gone, I saw my daughter so isolated. She didn't contribute to anything. She would just be there doing nothing, in tears, and any noise she would hear would make her just withdraw. We met with the superintendent and she said they were working on a plan and it took a couple of weeks, but they finally got a woman to come in and we absolutely love her. She's still in the classroom, which is wonderful, and the classroom actually got so much better. They are joking and being silly and all that.

JENN. After this all happened, we went to our synagogue. The rabbi said, "Is anybody from here? Does anybody have questions or does anybody have comments?" So I turned to my son and said, "Do you want me to say something?" and he was like, "No, no, no." And then he was like, "Yeah," and so I said, "This is my son. He was there. He survived." And everybody was just like, shocked, ya know, that I got up and said something. And so my six-year-old stands in front of the whole congregation and says, "Every day there are shadows, but every day there is also light too."

MICHAEL. I mean, it's amazing... I mean just...putting him down, putting him to bed at night. I check in on him before I get to bed and am just amazed at how much he's grown since December.

JULIE. That's one thing you see in children. They're so resilient. They're so much more resilient than we are, right? They're very happy kids, because kids are supposed to be happy. That's where the innocence comes from. You look out and you see his friends who were also affected and they're outside and all just boys playing football, you know? Doing what they're supposed to do.

JENN. Everything is blooming. It's gorgeous. And the contrast to what it felt like here on December fourteenth, is just, you know...it was so different. Things are blossoming. Life came back. It's coming back.

JOE. This all leaves you with a lot of questions and I don't think that's a bad thing. I don't because the more people are questioning, the more they're talking about it and the more they're thinking about, "Where do we go from here?" and, "What can we do from here?" and as an educator, "What can we learn from this?" That's so cliché, but it's true. What can we learn from this?

GEORGIA. There's – there's a journey to go through, ya know? You've got to go through the darkness before we can get to the light.

DARREN. This is still home and will continue to be. You see it with every tragedy. The president or the town officials say, "Well look, Houston, we're gonna get through this." In Florida, "We, as Floridians, are a tough bunch!" This gets said at any national tragedy. I know for us that's true...but more.

YOLIE. It's like all love is. It just...it draws things to you. And so, I feel like it's my duty 'cause this is how I am since I got here. You have to just let go and just be joyful and live joyfully because the alternative is and was misery.

CARLA. Just because you're a survivor doesn't mean you're a hundred percent. You should go away happy and you're fine. Get over it, shake it off. The kid is different. These parents lost something. Even though they still have their kids, they still lost something.

BILL. My love for this town was there long before this ever happened. When we bought this house, we saw eighty something houses. I was the biggest royal pain in the neck that you could ever think of.

CAROLE. Mmmhmm.

BILL. And finally, the realtor and my wife turn around and they stop the car in the middle of the road and they said, "Which one?"

CAROLE. Pick it!

BILL. And I said, "Okay. The white one with the fence."

CAROLE. Fine! The white one with the fence.

> *(They both share a laugh.)*

We're just moving up. We're going to help our families and continue our counseling. Take care of the cops and the EMTs and the dispatchers and the high school kids, and you know, hope we can heal and that it won't hurt so much. Newtown has to move on...

> *(To the* **CAST***.)*

So let's move on!

> *(We hear a guitar melody play, as the* **CAST** *grab erasers and chalk and begin to clean up and fix the chalk drawing of the town on the stage floor. They erase and redraw parts that may need it or that have been smudged and attempt to get it as close to the way it was in the first part of the play. They also erase all the words off the side chalkboards. Once finished,* **JENN** *stands center stage with a piece of chalk in her hands, offering it out.* **KAT** *grabs it first and heads to the wall chalkboard and writes "FAMILY.")*

KAT. Always was, always will be.

> *(***CHRIS*** walks to the wall and writes, "CONNECTED."* **DARREN** *walks to the wall and writes "HOPE.")*

JENN. *(Goes to the wall and begins to write, stops to say this and then writes her words.)* Can I say two? Wait... I wanna say three. Capital "S," Strong, period.
Capital "R," Resilient, period.
Capital "T," Transformative, period.

> *(***JENN*** hands the chalk to* **MICHAEL***, who writes, "STRENGTH,")*

(JERIANN and STARR walk to the wall and start writing. JERIANN writes, "FRIENDLY" and STARR writes "HUGGY." RABBI writes "NEW WORLD.")

CARLA. *(As she writes the word "COMPASSION.")* There is so much of it in this town. So much. I've never seen anything like it. I hope I never do again.

But there is so much.

(CAROLE and BILL walk over to the wall, CAROLE writes "L-O-" and BILL finishes it with a "V-E.")

MIKE. *(As he writes "TOGETHER.")* Because the only way you're going to push through and do it, is together. You can't be a one-man band. You can reflect back, but you have to move forward. You have to do it immediately and together.

(JULIE walks to the wall and writes "PERSEVERANCE," as CARRIE writes "HOME." YOLIE walks to the walls and looks them over. After a few beats she circles the word "LOVE.")

YOLIE. It's all about how you ripple out, and what these vibrations can be. We are love. We are Newtown. That message says it all.

(The whole CAST stands in the center of the stage, and we hear the sound of a pebble hitting water. The stage is then consumed in ripples of water lighting that flow out as far as possible. Blackout.)

End of Play

Music by John Wyeth
Lyrics by George Robinson

Come, Thou Fount Of Every Blessing

Come, Thou Fount Of Every Blessing - p.3

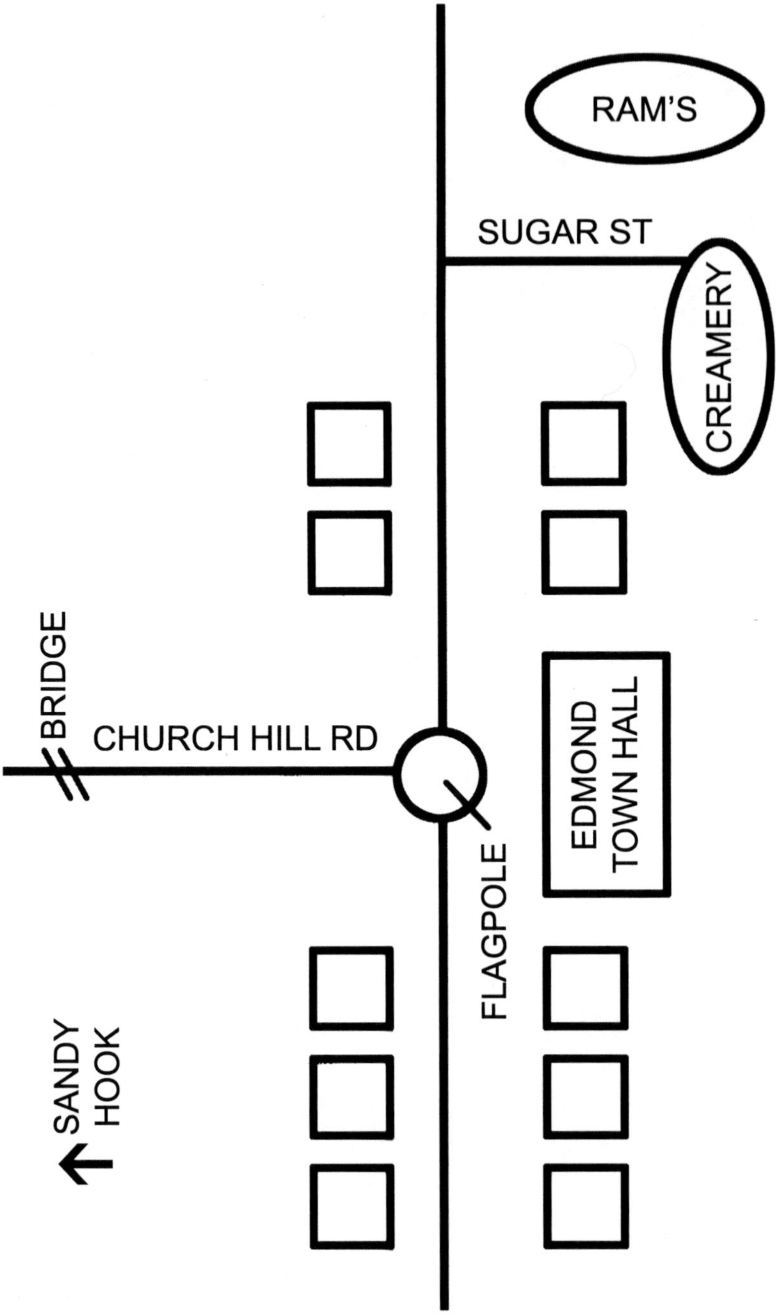
RAM'S
SUGAR ST
CREAMERY
BRIDGE
CHURCH HILL RD
EDMOND
TOWN HALL
FLAGPOLE
SANDY
HOOK